The Three Bears
Holiday Rhyme Book

Written by Jane Yolen

Illustrated by Jane Dyer

HARCOURT BRACE & COMPANY

San Diego   New York   London

To Brooke and Cecily, who were there
from the beginning of Baby Bear
—J. Y. and J. D.

Library of Congress Cataloging-in-Publication Data
Yolen, Jane.
The three bears holiday rhyme book/Jane Yolen; illustrated by Jane Dyer.—1st ed.
p.   cm.
Summary: A collection of fifteen poems depicting various holidays as they
might be celebrated by Goldilocks and the Three Bears.
ISBN 0-15-200932-9
1. Children's poetry, American.   2. Holidays—Juvenile poetry.
3. Bears—Juvenile poetry.   [1. Holidays—Poetry.   2. Bears—Poetry.
3. American poetry.]   I. Dyer, Jane, ill.   II. Title.
PS3575.043T45   1995   93–17252

Printed in Singapore

First edition
A B C D E

The illustrations in this book were done in Winsor and Newton watercolors
    and Rotring artist's colors on 140-lb. Waterford hot-press watercolor paper.
The display and text type were set in Adroit Light by
    Harcourt Brace & Company Photocomposition Center, San Diego, California.
Color separations by Bright Arts, Ltd., Singapore
Printed and bound by Tien Wah Press, Singapore
This book was printed with soya-based inks on Leykam recycled paper,
    which contains more than 20 percent postconsumer waste and
    has a total recycled content of at least 50 percent.
Production supervision by Warren Wallerstein and Cheryl Kennedy
Designed by Linda Lockowitz

Contents

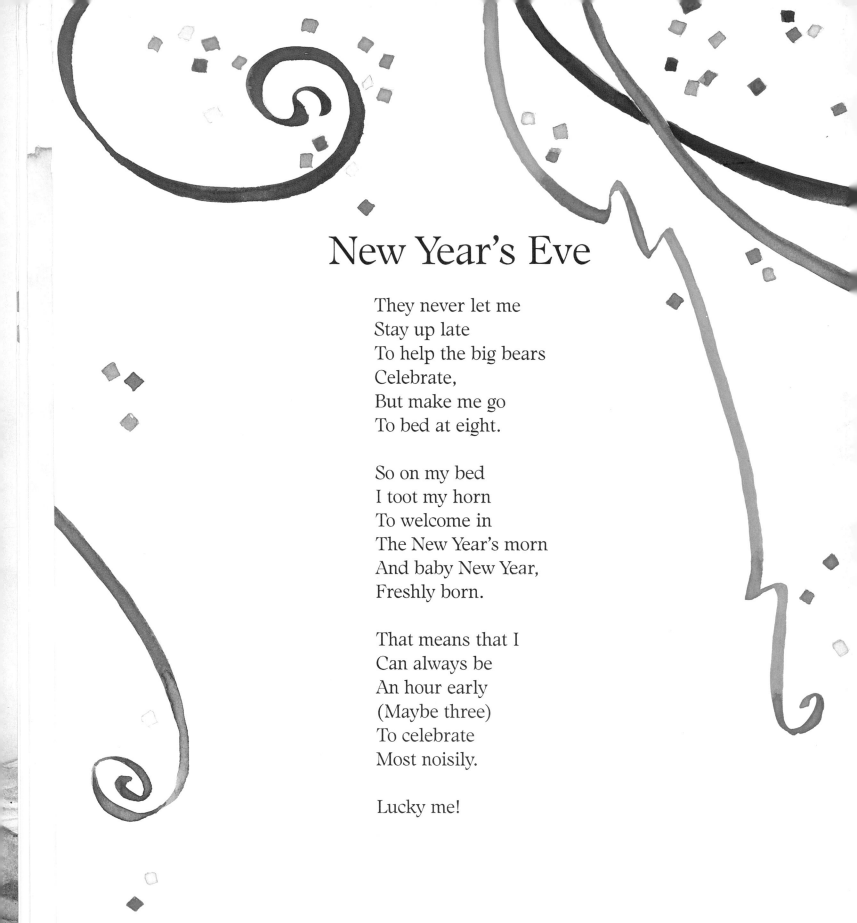

New Year's Eve

They never let me
Stay up late
To help the big bears
Celebrate,
But make me go
To bed at eight.

So on my bed
I toot my horn
To welcome in
The New Year's morn
And baby New Year,
Freshly born.

That means that I
Can always be
An hour early
(Maybe three)
To celebrate
Most noisily.

Lucky me!

Arbor Day

Do bears love trees?
They love them lots,
When birds lay eggs
Up in the tops.

Do bears love trees?
They love them very—
Apple trees and pear
And cherry.

And bears love trees
When bees are home,
The hollows filled
With honeycomb.

Do bears love trees?
Oh, sure bears do.
Since I'm a bear,
I love them, too.

16

May Day

Goldie's basket
Glows with reds.
Roses nod
Their velvet heads.
Tulips tip
With every breeze,
Trying very
Hard to please.

In my basket
Gold and green
Are the colors
To be seen.
Black-eyed Susans,
Daffodils,
Dandelions
From the hills.

Which is nicer
For the day?
Which is really
Right for May?
Goldie says that
Both are fine.
But don't you think
That you like mine?

17

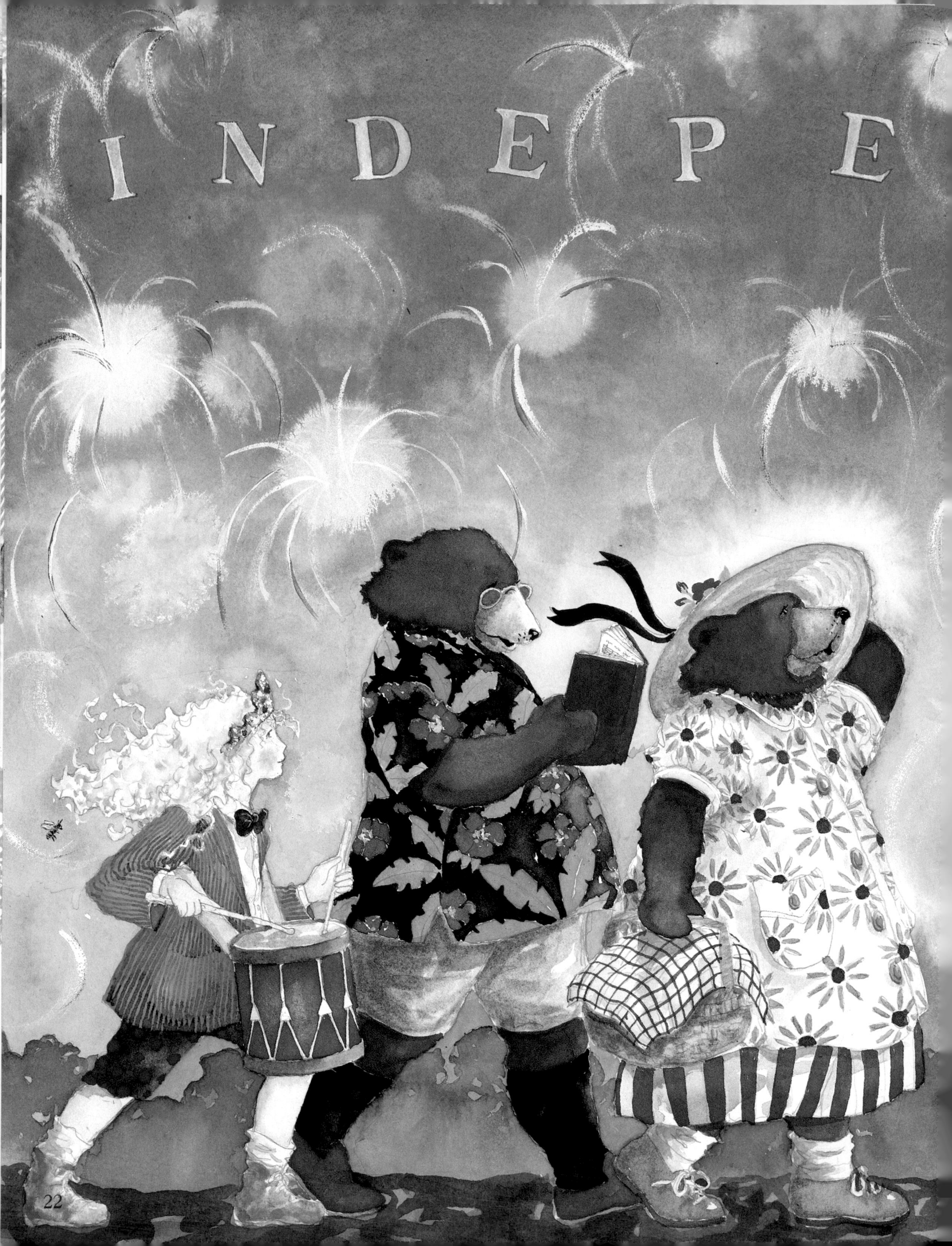
I N D E P E

Independence Day

Rockets write
Across the sky
INDEPENDENCE
Ten feet high.

Firecrackers
In the air,
Signaling
To Baby Bear.

Up above,
Let freedom ring;
Down below,
The bears all sing,

Caroling
A nation's song—
Ten feet high,
A lifetime long.

Halloween

When Goldie and I
Go trick-or-treat
At every house
On Forest Street

Our bags get full,
Our feet get sore,
But still we want
Just one treat more.

So why—when we
Have just come home
To share our cake
And honeycomb—

Are we too pooped
To eat at all?
We leave our bags
Out in the hall,

And fall asleep
Without a bite.
It happens every
Halloween night.

Thanksgiving

Thanks for forests,
Thanks for trees,
Special thanks
For honeybees.

Thanks for porridge,
Thanks for chairs—
Thanks for all
My special bears

Thanks for Goldie,
Once again,
Thanks from Baby Bear.
Amen.

Christmas & Chanukah

Stars are shining
Down the lane,
Making halos
On each pane.

Celebrations
For a night
Made of holy
Candlelight.

For each candle
Say a prayer.
Blessings on us,
Every bear.

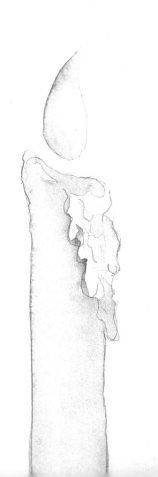

Happy Birthday

Here's the cake,
Candles lit.
Take a breath;
Think a bit.

Make a wish;
Blow with care.
Happy Birthday,
Baby Bear!

July 8, 1995

Happiest of Birthday wishes,
my dearest friends.
I hope with all my might
that it is a happy, healthy
year for you, Kathy.

Besides for the Happy Birthday
poem, my other favorite is "Earth
Day." I hope that you enjoy it!

I love you,
Marie